THE YEAR 2525

By

Mark Taylor

Table of Contents

Dedication

To the women I love.

Acknowledgment

I would like to thank everyone at the Book Publishing Company, in particular the art department, for their excellent work designing the book cover, and a special mention goes to Cheryl-Anne and Felix Larsson. Without their support and guidance, this work would never have been published.

About the Author

Mark Taylor is a new writer who likes to explore new ideas and is passionate about folklore.

Chapter 1 - Paragon's Plight

Paragon Prime stood at the edge of the playground, the wind carrying the faint sound of children's laughter from a distance. But his focus wasn't on them—it was on the invisible lines that divided the cracked asphalt and patched-up houses in the neighbourhood he once called home.

From his vantage point, he could see the markers of the unspoken boundaries. On one corner, a brightly painted mural celebrating one community's heritage; across the street, another mural, equally vibrant yet wholly separate in its imagery and story. The alleys between these blocks weren't just shortcuts—they were borders.

Paragon clenched his fists, his usually impassive face darkening with concern. His suit, a symbol of his ideals of unity and order, felt out of place here, like a sharp edge in a fragmented mirror.

"They coexist," he murmured to himself as if trying to convince the gnawing anxiety in his chest. And it was true—on the surface, the communities lived side by side in what appeared to be an uneasy truce. No open violence, no outward hostility. But Paragon saw the cracks beneath the façade. It wasn't integration. It was separation disguised as peace.

He strolled down the street, his gaze sweeping over the details. The corner store, once a communal gathering place, now had two separate entrances catering to "different crowds." The park benches were clustered unevenly, unintentionally segregating those who sat there. Even the faded graffiti on the walls told stories of rivalry, a quiet reminder of past conflicts that had never truly healed.

As he walked, a group of teenagers brushed past him, their laughter echoing down the street. But his sharp ears caught the edge of their conversation—a hushed remark about "them" and "us." He stopped in his tracks, his pulse quickening. Even the youth, the supposed hope for the future, carried the weight of division.

Paragon's chest tightened. He had dedicated his life to preserving peace and creating harmony through uniformity. And yet, here, in the heart of his own community, he saw only fractures. Subtle. Hidden. But fractures nonetheless. It was like standing on a frozen lake, aware of the cracks spidering beneath your feet, knowing that one wrong step could send you plunging into chaos.

He turned a corner and found himself in front of a dilapidated community centre. The paint was peeling, and the windows were boarded up, but the old sign above the door still read, "Unity in Diversity." He stared at the words, his jaw tightening. They felt hollow. A cruel joke. Diversity, to him, was a polite term for division—a polite term for conflict waiting to happen.

The sound of raised voices broke his thoughts. Across the street, two men stood arguing over something trivial—a parking spot, perhaps, or an accidental bump. But the aggression in their tone hinted at something deeper, something more dangerous. Paragon watched, frozen, as bystanders began to take sides, each aligning with their respective communities.

Before things could escalate, one of the men backed off, muttering under his breath as he walked away. The crowd dispersed, tension lingering in the air like smoke after a fire. Paragon let out a breath he hadn't realized he was holding.

This was why he was afraid. This was why he believed in a homogenous society. Not out of hatred but out of fear. Fear of the fragile peace shattering. Fear of the violence he had dedicated his life to avoiding. As he turned to leave, his reflection caught his eye in a shattered storefront window. For a moment, he saw himself not as a guardian of order but as a man caught between ideals and reality. The reflection blurred as his vision clouded with uncertainty.

"How do you unify what was never whole to begin with?" he whispered to no one.

And with that, he walked away, the weight of the question pressing down on him like a storm he could neither escape nor control.

Later that day, Paragon Prime sat alone in his study, the faint glow of a desk lamp illuminating the scattered papers and books that spoke to a lifetime of meticulous thought. The room smelled of aged leather and dust, remnants of a bygone world he clung to as if it might slip through his fingers at any moment.

On the desk lay an old photograph, its edges frayed with time. It showed a younger Paragon, smiling broadly, his arm draped over the shoulder of an equally youthful colleague. They stood on the steps of a university, a banner above them reading "Voices of Change: A Future United." He remembered that day vividly—the passion, the optimism, the belief that they could forge a better world through dialogue and innovation.

He sighed, running a calloused hand over his face. "Naïve," he muttered under his breath. "So damn naïve."

Outside the study's window, the city's lights twinkled in the darkness, a patchwork of communities pressed together like mismatched tiles on a floor that could crack at any moment. He had spent decades watching these communities grow—not together, but apart, like rivers carving divergent paths through the same land.

"They call it progress," he whispered bitterly, his voice filled with equal parts anger and sorrow. "But progress isn't a flood sweeping away the past—it's a stream, slowly eroding, shaping, building with time. Not this...this experiment."

He picked up a report from the corner of his desk, its cover stamped with the words "Behavioural Insights Division: Strategies for Social Cohesion." He flipped through the pages, his eyes scanning the carefully worded recommendations. Nudge Theory, they called it. Subtle adjustments to steer people's thoughts, beliefs, and behaviours without them realizing it. Elegant in its simplicity. Insidious in its purpose.

Paragon slammed the report shut. "Patronizing drivel," he growled. "They think themselves architects of a harmonious future, but all they're doing is painting over the cracks. A fresh coat of optimism on a crumbling foundation."

He rose from his chair, pacing the room. His mind turned to history, to the stories he had studied and lived through. Yugoslavia. Iraq. Places where disparate peoples had been forced together, their shared histories overshadowed by differences too vast to reconcile overnight. "Authoritarianism held them together," he mused aloud, "until it didn't. And then, chaos. Civil war. Blood in the streets."

His pacing slowed, and he rested a hand on the windowsill, gazing out at the city. The influx of cultures and identities over the past twenty-five years had reshaped everything—he could see it in the food stalls lining the streets and hear it in the cacophony of languages in the marketplace. Part of him, the younger Paragon, might have celebrated it. But the older Paragon saw only the fractures.

"Stories hold us together," he murmured, almost wistfully. "Shared memories. A collective past. Not slogans written by committees or theories crafted in boardrooms."

A knock at the door broke his reverie. It was his assistant, a young idealist fresh out of university. "Sir, the council is ready for your input on the social integration policy."

Paragon turned, his expression weary but resolute. "Integration," he echoed, the word heavy with meaning. "They don't even understand what it means. It's not something you enforce—it's something that grows, slowly, like roots intertwining over time."

His assistant hesitated. "Should I tell them you'll be there?"

Paragon considered for a moment, then shook his head. "No. Let them play their games of nudges and narratives. I've said my piece, and they don't listen. They don't want to listen."

The assistant nodded, though their expression betrayed disappointment. As they left, Paragon returned to the window, watching the city lights flicker. For a moment, he allowed himself to imagine a different future— one where the advocates of change tempered their zeal with patience, where progress was built on understanding rather than imposition.

But the moment passed, and reality settled in like a familiar weight. "They'll learn," he muttered. "One way or another."

The glow of the screen illuminated Paragon Prime's weathered face, his fingers hovering over the keyboard as he reread the words he'd typed. The tweet was simple and honest—a lament for what he saw as a lost harmony, a criticism of policies he believed were increasingly authoritarian, and a questioning of the government's self-proclaimed advocacy for democracy.

He hesitated for only a moment before hitting "Post." It wasn't anger that drove him—it was conviction, the belief that someone needed to speak the truth as he saw it. He leaned back in his chair, staring at the screen as notifications began to appear. Likes. Retweets. Comments. The ripple he'd created was beginning to spread.

Hours later, as he was preparing for bed, the knock came. Sharp. Authoritative. Paragon froze, his heart pounding. He moved to the window and peered out into the night. Blue lights flashed on the street below, casting ominous shadows against the walls of his home. A group of officers stood at his door.

The knock came again, louder this time.

Paragon opened the door slowly, his face calm but his mind racing. The lead officer, a tall man with a rigid posture, stepped forward. "Paragon Prime, you are under arrest for violating the Communications Conduct Act, specifically for inciting discord and undermining public trust in government policies."

Paragon blinked, his voice steady despite the storm of emotions building within him. "I expressed an opinion. That's not a crime."

The officer's expression didn't waver. "Your statement has been deemed harmful to social cohesion and in violation of community standards. You have the right to remain silent."

Before Paragon could respond, two officers stepped past him into the house, moving with precision as they seized his computer and phone.

He watched in silence, his mind flashing back to a younger version of himself—one who had championed free speech, who had believed in the power of dialogue to bridge divides. That belief now felt like a distant dream.

As they led him out into the night, his neighbours peered through their windows, their faces a mixture of curiosity and fear. The city's lights seemed harsher than usual, their glow casting long, accusatory shadows.

The patrol car door slammed shut behind him, and for the first time, Paragon allowed himself a moment of doubt. Had he miscalculated? Had his words, however heartfelt, painted him as a relic of the past rather than a voice of reason?

The car pulled away, its engine humming softly as it carried him toward an uncertain future. Outside, the city continued to pulse with life, oblivious to the man who had once dedicated himself to its peace and unity.

In the silence of the car, Paragon closed his eyes. The glow of the screen still lingered in his mind, a faint reminder of the words he could never take back.

At the re-education centre, Paragon leaned back in his chair, the cold metal pressing against his spine. His fingers trembled slightly—not with fear but with frustration. "You call this respect and dignity," he said, his voice low, controlled, "but this—this room, these questions—it's all a performance. A way to reframe my convictions as flaws."

Dr. Vren rested her clasped hands on the desk between them, her face a mask of measured neutrality. "Convictions can be admirable," she said calmly. "But they must evolve with the world. A rigid belief system, no matter how deeply held, can become a barrier to progress."

Paragon's lips twitched into a bitter smile. "Progress. Your favourite word. Tell me, Dr. Vren, what does progress mean to you? Forcing people to accept change they never asked for, dictated by a minority who think they know best?"

Dr. Vren tilted her head as if weighing his words. "Progress," she replied, "means striving toward a society where everyone— regardless of background, identity, or culture—has the opportunity to thrive. Yes, change can be uncomfortable, but discomfort often precedes growth."

Paragon's throat tightened. "Spare me the platitudes. I was like you once—an optimist, a believer in the power of change. But I've lived long enough to see the cracks beneath your vision. You don't create harmony by erasing the past. By ignoring the narratives that have held societies together for centuries."

Dr. Vren's gaze softened, but her voice remained steady. "No one is erasing the past, Paragon. We honour it by learning from it. Societies that fail to adapt stagnate—and stagnation breeds its own form of chaos."

Paragon leaned forward, his eyes sharp. "And what about the chaos you're creating now? The fractures you're papering over with theories and slogans? Yugoslavia. Iraq. Do those names mean anything to you? Societies thrown together overnight, held together only by force—and when that force was gone, they tore themselves apart."

Dr. Vren's expression didn't waver, but her fingers tightened around her clasped hands. "And yet, here we are," she said softly. "You and I, sitting across from each other, engaging in dialogue. Isn't that proof that a diverse society can find common ground?"

Paragon's laugh was hollow. "This isn't dialogue. It's coercion dressed up as conversation. You bring me here, strip away my freedom, and then tell me to embrace yours. That's not harmony. It's tyranny."

Dr. Vren took a deep breath, leaning back in her chair. "I understand your frustration," she said. "And I won't pretend that we have all the answers. But tell me this, Paragon: in your ideal world, where everyone conforms to the same narrative, what happens to individuality? To creativity? To the spark that drives humanity forward?"

For a moment, Paragon faltered. The question hung in the air like a challenge. He thought of his younger self, the dreamer who had once welcomed new ideas with open arms. But that same self had also believed in caution, in patience, in building bridges rather than burning them.

"Individuality," he said finally, "thrives when it's tempered by responsibility. Creativity flourishes within boundaries. Without structure, without shared stories and values, you have anarchy."

Dr. Vren met his gaze, her expression unreadable. "And without openness to change," she countered, "you have stagnation.

Somewhere between the two lies balance. That's what we're striving for."

Paragon didn't respond. He sat in silence, the weight of his own thoughts pressing down on him. He wasn't convinced—not yet. But a part of him, buried deep beneath years of scepticism, wondering if perhaps, just perhaps, there was a glimmer of truth in her words.

Dr. Vren sighed, a trace of sadness flickering across her composed face. "It must be exhausting," she said quietly.

Paragon frowned. "What?"

"Carrying the weight of perfection," she explained. "Do you ever wonder what it might feel like to let go of control? To allow the unpredictable into your life?"

For a split second, something flickered in his eyes—doubt, perhaps, or curiosity—but it was gone as quickly as it came. He straightened his posture, his voice cold. "I don't need your pity."

"This isn't pity," Dr. Vren said, standing up. "It's an invitation. The door to understanding is always open, Paragon. You just have to choose to walk through it."

She left him alone in the room, her footsteps echoing down the hallway. Paragon sat in silence, staring at the blank walls. For the first time in years, his mind felt… unsettled. He didn't like it.

The days that followed were a blur of monotony. Paragon was subjected to lectures, group discussions, and carefully curated exercises designed to challenge his worldview. The re-education centre was a sterile place, devoid of colour or warmth as if to strip its inhabitants of any sense of individuality. Yet, it was the one-on-one session with Dr. Vren that lingered in his mind.

Their second meeting began much like the first. Paragon sat rigidly in the chair, his arms crossed, his expression guarded. Dr. Vren, ever composed, studied him for a moment before speaking.

"Tell me, Paragon," she began, "what does freedom mean to you?"

He scoffed. "Freedom is the absence of control. It's the ability to think, speak, and act without interference."

Dr. Vren tilted her head, her gaze piercing. "And yet, here you are. A symbol of freedom, confined. Do you think your definition is complete?"

Paragon's jaw tightened. "I'm here because I spoke the truth. That doesn't make me any less free."

"Doesn't it?" she pressed. "True freedom, I believe, is found in connection—in understanding and being understood."

He shook his head, frustration bubbling to the surface. "You speak in riddles, Doctor. Connection in your world is just another word for control. It's a way to bind people to a belief system not necessarily of their choosing, to strip them of their individuality."

Dr. Vren leaned forward, her voice soft but firm. "Connection in my world doesn't erase individuality, Paragon. It enhances it. When we share our stories, we find strength—not in conformity, but in unity. Isn't that what you once fought for?"

Her words struck a nerve. Paragon looked away, his thoughts a whirlwind of doubt and defiance. He had always prided himself on his clarity of purpose and his unwavering belief in his ideals. But now, cracks were beginning to form in the foundation of his convictions.

Dr. Vren didn't push further. She simply sat in silence, giving him the space to wrestle with his thoughts. After a long pause, she spoke again.

"Change is never easy," she said gently. "But it's necessary. The world you envision, the unity you seek—it can't be built on rigid ideals. It requires flexibility, empathy, and yes, a willingness to let go of control."

Paragon didn't respond. But as he left the room, a single question echoed in his mind: What if she was right?

The next meeting, Paragon entered the sterile room, its familiar coldness gnawing at the edges of his nerves. But as his gaze met Dr. Vren's, something softened. Her presence, once simply professional and composed, now carried an inexplicable warmth—a strange solace in an otherwise oppressive place.

She looked up from her tablet, a small, almost involuntary smile curving her lips. "Paragon," she greeted, her voice softer than he remembered. "How are you feeling today?"

"Still breathing," he replied, his usual gruffness tinged with a subtle, almost teasing tone. He eased into the chair across from her, his broad shoulders filling the space. For a moment, neither spoke, the silence charged with unspoken thoughts.

Dr. Vren set the tablet aside, folding her hands neatly in her lap. "I've been reviewing your progress," she began, though her voice faltered slightly. "You've been more… reflective in your recent interactions at the centre."

Paragon leaned back, his piercing eyes studying her. "That's one way of putting it. Guess I've had a lot to think about."

She nodded, though her thoughts seemed elsewhere. "You remind me of someone," she admitted after a pause, her words uncharacteristically personal. "My father."

Paragon raised an eyebrow, his rugged features momentarily betraying his curiosity. "Your father?"

She hesitated as if weighing how much to reveal. "He was... strong, principled. But distant. Always carrying the weight of the world on his shoulders. It made him admirable, but also... lonely."

Her words struck a chord deeper than Paragon expected. He shifted in his seat, his usual stoicism giving way to a rare vulnerability. "Sounds familiar," he muttered, more to himself than to her.

Dr. Vren tilted her head, her gaze softening. "You don't have to carry it alone, you know. Whatever it is you're holding onto."

Paragon's laugh was low, almost self-deprecating. "Easier said than done, Doctor. Letting people in—it's not exactly my strong suit."

"Maybe it doesn't have to be," she countered gently. "Maybe it's enough to start with... one person."

The room seemed to shrink around them, the walls fading into the background as their connection deepened. Paragon found himself holding her gaze longer than he intended, a flicker of something unfamiliar sparking between them—something he couldn't quite name.

Dr. Vren's cheeks flushed slightly, but she didn't look away. "You are my most challenging case," she admitted with a faint smile. "But also the most intriguing."

"And you," Paragon replied, his voice softer than usual, "have been the only thing keeping me sane in this place."

For a brief, suspended moment, the barriers they had both carefully maintained seemed to dissolve. But as quickly as it came, the moment passed, each retreating behind their respective walls. Yet the air between them was undeniably changed, charged with a new and unspoken understanding.

Their next session began with an almost palpable tension in the air. Paragon entered the room, his usual stoic demeanour intact, but there was a flicker of something else in his eyes—an unease, or perhaps anticipation. Dr. Vren, seated at her usual spot, looked up as he approached. She seemed more composed than he felt, but even she couldn't completely mask the slight quickening of her breath.

"Paragon," she greeted, her voice carrying the same warmth that had become his anchor in this place. "How are you today?"

He shrugged, a faint smirk tugging at the corner of his mouth. "Still here. I suppose that counts for something."

She chuckled softly, the sound breaking through the otherwise clinical atmosphere. "I'll take that as progress."

For the first few moments, they followed their usual routine—discussing his thoughts, his reflections on the lectures, and his interpretations of the centre's teachings. But as the minutes ticked by, their conversation began to drift, becoming less structured and more personal.

"You know," Dr. Vren said suddenly, her voice hesitant, "you remind me of why I chose this work in the first place."

Paragon raised an eyebrow, his rugged face betraying a hint of curiosity. "Is that so?"

She nodded, her fingers fidgeting slightly with the edge of her notebook. "I've always believed that people, no matter how set in their ways, have the capacity for growth—for change. And with you..." She paused, searching for the right words. "It's like watching a mountain shift. Slow, almost imperceptible, but undeniably powerful."

He leaned back in his chair, her words sinking in. For a man who had spent decades guarding his emotions, her observation felt strangely disarming. "I didn't think I was much of an inspiration," he admitted, his voice low.

"You'd be surprised," she replied, her gaze steady. "Even the most stubborn of mountains can reveal hidden beauty, given the right conditions."

Paragon's lips twitched into a rare smile, one that softened his weathered features. "And here I thought you were trying to tame me."

"Taming you would be impossible," she said with a playful glint in her eye. "And besides, that's not my goal. I'm more interested in understanding you."

Their eyes met, and for a moment, the room seemed to shrink around them. The clinical walls and the oppressive weight of the centre faded into the background, leaving only the two of them. There was an undeniable pull between them, a connection that neither could fully articulate, but both felt keenly.

Dr. Vren broke the silence, her cheeks flushing slightly. "This... dynamic," she began, her voice faltering. "It's unusual. But I think it's important."

Paragon nodded slowly, his expression thoughtful. "Unusual doesn't mean bad," he said, his voice softer than she'd ever heard it.

She smiled a genuine, unguarded smile that lit up her face. "No," she agreed. "It doesn't."

As the session came to an end, neither of them moved right away. The unspoken understanding between them lingered, heavy with possibilities and uncertainties. When Paragon finally stood, he hesitated for a brief moment before speaking.

"Thank you," he said, his tone earnest. "For... everything."

Dr. Vren looked up at him, her own barriers momentarily lowered. "You're welcome, Paragon. And thank you—for reminding me why this work matters."

He left the room then, but the connection they had shared remained, a thread that tied them together in ways neither fully understood. And as Dr. Vren watched him go, she couldn't help but wonder if perhaps, in helping him find his path, she was finding her own as well.

As the meetings went on, Paragon began to notice the quiet tension in Dr. Vren's eyes. He'd seen those eyes shift over their sessions from unwavering confidence in her mission to something more conflicted— uncertainty, perhaps, or even defiance.

Paragon started to become a little bolder in his approach to Dr Vren. "This centre," Paragon said, his voice low and measured, "isn't about unity. It's about control. You know that."

Dr. Vren hesitated, her fingers curling around the edge of her notebook. "Paragon, we've been over this. The goal is to create balance—"

"Balance?" He cut her off, leaning forward with an intensity that made her breath catch. "Is it balance when people are stripped of their voices? When dissent is crushed under the guise of harmony?"

Her instinct was to push back, to defend the system she had dedicated her life to. But the conviction in his gaze, the sheer force of his words, made something inside her waver. "And what would you propose instead?" she asked, her voice quieter now.

"Freedom," he said simply. "Real freedom. Where people can think for themselves."

Dr. Vren's lips pressed into a thin line. "Freedom without responsibility leads to chaos. You know that as well as I do."

"Maybe," he admitted, his tone softening. "But this isn't responsibility. This is fear dressed up as order. And I think you're starting to see that."

The words hung in the air between them, daring her to deny their truth. For the first time, Dr. Vren felt the full weight of her doubts—the gnawing sense that perhaps the system she served was not as just as she'd believed.

In the weeks that followed, their conversations began to shift. Dr. Vren became more candid, sharing glimpses of her own frustrations and fears. Paragon, in turn, opened up about the ideals he had once fought for and the disillusionment that followed. Slowly, a fragile trust began to form between them—a bond forged in shared doubt and the spark of something more.

It was late one evening, after their official session had ended that Dr. Vren made a decision that would change everything. She lingered in the room as Paragon stood to leave, her voice stopping him in his tracks.

She took a deep breath, her gaze meeting his, steady now despite the vulnerability etched across her face. "I don't know if this is right or what it even means, but I can't deny it anymore. I feel something for you, something I never expected to feel in a place like this. And I don't know where it will lead, but... I had to tell you."

For a moment, they stood in silence, the enormity of what she had just done hanging between them. Then, slowly, Paragon nodded. "You realize there's no turning back from this."

Dr. Vren leaned back, determination flickering in her eyes. "If the system won't change, then I'll work within it. I can argue for your release on the grounds that you've reformed, that you've embraced the principles we preach here."

Paragon frowned. "And what about you? If they suspect—"

"I'll be careful," she interrupted firmly. "This isn't just about you, Paragon. It's about us. If we can't change the system, then at least we can have a life together outside of it."

He didn't respond immediately, his mind racing with thoughts of hope and guilt. It felt like a betrayal of his former self, but for the first time in years, he allowed himself to hope—not for a past that was lost, but for a life worth living.

In the weeks that followed, Dr. Vren began to subtly advocate for his release. She framed her arguments carefully, presenting him as a success story of the centre's methods—a man who had seen the error of his ways and embraced a new path. It was a delicate balance, one that required all of her wit and cunning. But slowly, the walls around him began to loosen.

The day of his release came quietly, with no fanfare or ceremony. As Paragon stepped out into the open air for the first time in years, Dr. Vren was there, waiting for him. She smiled, and for the first time in as long as he could remember, he felt a warmth he thought he had lost forever.

"What now?" he asked, his voice rough but hopeful.

"Now," she said, slipping her hand into his, "we start over. Together." And as they walked away from the centre, leaving behind the weight of the past, they knew that while the world remained unchanged, they had found something worth holding onto: each other.

Chapter 2 – The Year 2125

The year was 2125, and the world had been reshaped by a century of tumultuous change. Towering cities of shimmering metal and glass stretched toward a dusky sky, their lights dimmed by layers of smog and forgotten dreams. A relentless march of progress had left little room for remembrance, erasing the past to pave an uncertain future. This was the age Matthew Levy had lived to see, though it was not the world he had hoped for.

Matthew's sixtieth birthday passed in quiet solitude, unmarked by celebration. Once a member of a race renowned for its unparalleled achievements and innovation—a race that had, at its height, wielded immense power—he now stood as a relic of a history most would rather forget. His people, once architects of prosperity, had dwindled to the shadows of society. From commanding nearly a third of the globe's population and ninety percent of its wealth, they now made up less than two percent, their influence a faint echo.

For Matthew, the descent into obscurity was not just history—it was his life. He was born into a world where his race had begun to fall, their achievements vilified, their stories rewritten, their monuments torn down. The decline began when a minority within Matthew's race became emotionally attached to the concept of equality to the point of neurosis. They felt it was unfair that their race, although in a minority, controlled nearly all the wealth. These individuals were too unpopular to be elected, so they infiltrated government institutions, particularly those connected to education. Their goal was to indoctrinate the young with a narrative that their ancestors were morally wrong and that recompense and a perceived injustice should be righted. As this narrative took hold, monuments were destroyed, cultural artifacts erased, and the truth buried deep.

By the time Matthew reached adulthood, their narrative had been twisted into one of oppression, greed, and arrogance. And as other races filled the vacuum of power, his people had been left behind. The truth was buried deeper still, alongside the shattered remnants of a once-great legacy.

Now, Matthew had dedicated his life to the pursuit of that truth. Over decades, he had risked everything to uncover hidden records— evidence of his people's brilliance and cultural legacy. Yet his mission had branded him a fugitive, harassed by authorities who saw his work as defiance and rebellion. In his sixtieth year, he reflected on the choices that had shaped his path, the sacrifices he had made, and the faint hope that his actions might spark a better understanding of the past.

The air was heavy, laden with the weight of unspoken stories and forgotten voices as Matthew stood amidst the broken marble of a destroyed cultural landmark. This monument once celebrated his race's achievements. The ruins of the monument stood desolate, silent witnesses to a past erased. Its jagged edges jutted against the horizon, a ghostly reminder of what once was. Matthew had visited this place many times, drawn by the echoes of his people's stolen history, but never before had he encountered one of the men who embodied the cultural revolution that had torn it all down.

Oscar Ashworth was twenty-five years his senior. The man had once been a firebrand—a leading figure in the liberal revolution who had rewritten the narrative of their shared past. His speeches had stirred hearts, his ideals had galvanized action, and his influence had helped dismantle the legacy of dominance their race once held. But years of disillusionment had worn him down, and the fire in his voice had long since dimmed. Now, he was known to linger here, lost in the melancholy of how profoundly he had been mistaken, as though haunted by the ruins of both the monument and his ideals.

For years, Matthew had heard rumours of his presence, whispers that he frequented this place in quiet reflection. Yet, try as he might, Matthew had never been able to find him until now. The faint crunch of footsteps on shattered stone broke the heavy silence, and Matthew turned. There he was at last—a man whose actions had done as much as any to change the fortunes of his race and whose regret now mirrored Matthew's own anger.

Their eyes met, and for a brief moment, neither spoke. The weight of the years hung between them like an unspoken truth, too heavy to break easily.

"So, you've found me. I thought you might, eventually." His voice heavy with regret, eyes darting to the wreckage around them.

"Yes, I have found you. The man who helped tear down everything that mattered."

Oscar winced but held his ground, the weight of years pressing down on him. "I didn't erase the truth, Matthew. I believed I was freeing it— liberating others from a history of oppression. I didn't think it would end like this." He paused, his voice faltering as he struggled to meet Matthew's eyes. The silence hung between them, thick with unspoken accusations and mutual pain.

"I... I was mistaken."

"Mistaken? Is that what you call it? You rewrote history to paint our people as villains, destroyed monuments, erased centuries of achievements. Now, we're the ones oppressed, hunted, erased. Was that your idea of justice?"

"I didn't want this. None of us did. We thought the world would balance itself—we believed humanity could rise above its greed and hunger for power. But humanity… it doesn't change so easily." They shift uncomfortably, their gaze falling to the rubble at their feet.

"I was wrong."

"And what? That's supposed to absolve you? A simple 'I was wrong,' while the legacy of our people crumbles and fades into obscurity?" His frustration spilling over, cutting through Oscar's fragile defences.

"You're right to hate me. I hate myself, too. But what I did—what we did— it wasn't out of malice. It was out of hope. A foolish, misguided hope. If I could go back and undo it all, I would… but I can't." His voice broke, revealing a deep sorrow.

Matthew's anger burned brightly, his voice shaking with emotion as he took a step closer to Oscar. The ruins around them seemed to hold their breath, waiting for the weight of their words to settle.

"Hope?" Matthew's voice dripped with disdain. "What hope do we have now? Our people are hunted and erased from history as if we were nothing. And you—you believed you could rewrite humanity itself, that your ideals were enough to overcome greed, fear, and power. Tell me, Oscar, how did that turn out for you?"

Oscar flinched, his shoulders slumping under the burden of Matthew's words. "I don't expect forgiveness, Matthew. I know what

I've done. I see it every day in the faces of our people. I didn't understand the cost back then. None of us did. We thought we were building something better, but instead, we let the same cycle consume us."

Oscar lifted his gaze, his expression a fragile mixture of regret and defiance. "We thought we could change the nature of humanity, Matthew. We thought we could create fairness and equality—something lasting. But we underestimated the depth of fear and greed in people's hearts. We shattered the old order, only to watch a worse one rise in its place."

Matthew's fists clenched, his voice cutting through the thick air like a blade. "And in the process, you destroyed the only protection we had. Our history, our culture, our legacy—all sacrificed to your naïve dream."

Oscar nodded slowly, accepting the condemnation. "You're right. I thought we were doing what was necessary. I thought we were paving the way for a brighter future. But all we did was erase the past, not realizing that without it, there's no foundation for the future."

Matthew took another step forward, his anger simmering just below the surface. "You didn't just erase the past—you erased us. Our people are shadows now, hunted and forgotten, while you linger here and wallow in your mistakes. Why? Why do you come here, Oscar? To mourn what you've done? To face what little remains of the world you broke?"

Oscar's shoulders sagged, his eyes flickering back to the ruins. "I come here because it's the only place that still feels real to me. These stones, these ruins—they remind me of the weight of what we destroyed. I thought I was fighting for humanity, but all I've done is leave scars on it."

Matthew's voice rose, filled with a dangerous intensity. "Scars heal, Oscar. But what you did wasn't a wound that can heal—it was an amputation. You helped sever our people from power and re-write our place in history, and now you stand here and call it a mistake?"

Oscar lowered his head, the weight of Matthew's words pressing down on him. At 85 years old, he was a man hollowed by regret, his body frail and his spirit fractured. The fire of his youth, the conviction that had driven him to change the world, had long since burned out. All that remained were the ashes of his mistakes and the realization that he could never undo the damage.

"You're right, Matthew," Oscar said finally, his voice trembling with the weariness of decades. "I am powerless. I have been for years. The future I wanted to create was devoured by greed, fear, and ambition—just as history should have warned me. And now, there's nothing left of me but regret."

Matthew's anger faltered for a moment, replaced by a flicker of something more complex—pity, perhaps, or disgust at the man's resignation. He stepped closer, his expression unyielding. "If you're so powerless, then why are you still here? Why come to this place? Do you think wallowing in the ruins absolves you of your sins?"

Oscar's eyes lifted, meeting Matthew's gaze with surprising clarity. "No. It doesn't absolve me. Nothing ever will. I come here because… because I need to remember. If I don't feel the weight of what I did, who will? Who will carry that burden when I'm gone?" He gestured weakly to the rubble around them. "This place—it's all that's left of what I helped to destroy. And soon, even that will be gone."

Matthew's jaw tightened, the conflict within him growing. He despised Oscar for what he had done, for the irreversible loss inflicted on his people. But there was something deeply human in the man's despair, something that echoed his own longing to preserve a dying legacy.

Chapter 3 – The Year 2525

The sterile hum of the incubation chambers filled the air, a symphony of progress in a world where nature had long been rewritten. Beneath the artificial glow of the Biolabs, humanity thrived in ways once deemed impossible—children born without mothers, their genetic blueprints tailored to perfection. Aaliyah moved through the corridors unnoticed, her frail frame a relic of a bygone era. She carried with her the weight of a secret, one that pulsed faintly in the depths of her being, defying the sterile perfection that surrounded her. The world had forgotten what she represented, but she had not.

Aaliyah's memories were a mosaic of triumph and sorrow, each piece a testament to a life lived on the edge of extinction. Once celebrated as the last female born of natural birth, she had been a symbol of resilience and defiance. In her youth, she had stood at the forefront of a movement, her voice rising above the clamour of a world hurtling toward artificial perfection. She had fought for the sanctity of natural births, knowing that without the necessity of a menstrual cycle and with the power to choose a child's sex would one day make her gender obsolete. The world had increasingly become uninterested in her concerns. Now, in her one-hundred and thirtieth year, she carried the weight of that foresight, a burden as heavy as the silence that surrounded her.

Aaliyah's thoughts drifted to the echoes of history, to the stories of civilizations and identities that had faded into obscurity. She couldn't help but draw a parallel between her own existence and the end of the white race. A chapter closed two centuries ago through the quiet forces of time, choice, and change. The weight of her fears pressed heavily on her—would women, too, become largely forgotten from the annals of history? She felt the crushing responsibility of remembrance, of ensuring that the essence of womanhood would not vanish into the void of progress. The sterile world around her seemed indifferent, its perfection a stark contrast to the messy, beautiful imperfection of what once was.

Aaliyah's mind wandered back to her schooling, where she had learned about the groundbreaking work of Jie Chen, a name etched into the annals of human progress. Chen had been the trailblazer who, in the early 21st century, first achieved the creation of a fertilized embryo using the cells from two male mice. It was a discovery that had ignited waves of both awe and controversy, a scientific milestone that reshaped the trajectory of reproduction itself. Aaliyah acknowledged Chen's brilliance, even though, as a child, she had always resented it. Now, centuries later, she lived in the shadow of those advancements, haunted by the knowledge that they had played a part in erasing the very essence of what she represented.

Aaliyah's thoughts turned to the battles she had waged, the protests and pleas that had fallen on deaf ears. She had fought tirelessly to preserve her gender, to remind the world of the beauty and balance that women brought to humanity. But her efforts had been no match for the tide of eugenics, a relentless pursuit of bodies engineered for strength and speed. The world had become a place dominated by testosterone, where the ideals of perfection and sexual hedonism left no room for the delicate intricacies of Motherhood. Aaliyah had stood as a lone voice in a cacophony of progress. Her warnings were drowned out by the roar of a future that had no place for her kind. Now, as she had lived through a world shaped by those choices, she felt the weight of her failure, a quiet ache that echoed in the sterile silence around her.

The sterile white walls of the hospital room seemed to close in around Aaliyah as she lay in her bed, her breaths shallow and laboured. Dr. Makena-Vren sat beside her, his expression calm but tinged with a quiet reverence for the moment.

"You know," Aaliyah began, her voice barely above a whisper, "I always wondered if it would feel like this—like fading into a forgotten story."

Dr. Makena-Vren hesitated, his gaze fixed on the floor. "You're not forgotten, Aaliyah. You're a part of history, a chapter that shaped the world we live in now."

She managed a faint smile, her frail hand trembling as she reached for his. "History doesn't remember the chapters, it tears them out. It rewrites them, smooths over the edges, and pretends they were never there."

He nodded, his grip firm but gentle. "I won't pretend to understand what this means to you. I've lived in a world where women have always been a rarity, where progress was measured in numbers and outcomes, not in the lives we left behind."

Aaliyah's eyes glistened, her voice growing steadier despite her weakening body. "You see it as progress, don't you? The perfection of humanity, the elimination of what you call inefficiencies. But perfection is a cold, hollow thing, Doctor. It doesn't breathe, it doesn't love, it doesn't mourn."

Dr. Makena-Vren's expression softened, a flicker of doubt crossing his face. "I don't mourn, Aaliyah, but I do respect. You've carried the weight of something none of us can truly understand. And now, as you leave us, I realize the significance of this moment."

She closed her eyes for a moment, her voice now barely audible. "Promise me one thing, Doctor. Don't let them forget. Even if it's just a whisper in the wind, let them remember."

Dr. Makena-Vren's voice was steady, though his heart felt heavy. "I promise, Aaliyah. I'll remember."

As Aaliyah's consciousness slipped further into the void, fragments of her past danced before her eyes—memories of resistance, fleeting victories, and the weight of knowing the world had chosen perfection over presence. She recalled a passage from an obscure book she'd once read, salvaged from the hidden corners of the dark net. Another story of a vanishing people struck a chord, a haunting parallel to her own fate. With her final breath, as the sterile hum of the machines marked her passing, the words resonated in her mind, an epitaph for her existence: she was the last of the Mohicans.

Chapter 4 – The Year 2925

Max settles into his favourite chair, gesturing enthusiastically. "So, Leah, the multiverse theory is essentially the idea that there are countless parallel universes coexisting alongside our own. These universes could differ in tiny, almost imperceptible ways, or they could be wildly different. Imagine a universe where dinosaurs never went extinct and humans coexist with giant reptiles. Or another where the white race is no longer the dominant force. There's even the possibility of a universe where gravity works differently, and everything floats!"

Leah tilts her head, intrigued. "And how does this happen? Why would there be all these alternate realities?"

Max grins. "Well, scientists theorize it's linked to quantum mechanics— the tiniest building blocks of our reality. Whenever a decision is made, or an event occurs, the universe could 'split' to explore each possible outcome. For instance, in one universe, you decided to wear blue today. In another, you picked red. And then there's the crazy idea that every possible outcome of every choice creates its own universe. Infinite possibilities!" There could even be a universe where breakthroughs in the science of procreation— prohibited in the late 21st century—led to a world entirely devoid of women.

Leah narrows her eyes, a sly smile creeping onto her lips. "No women, huh? Sounds like a universe doomed to chaos and questionable fashion choices. I'd love to see how you handle a world without us. Spoiler alert: it's probably not great."

Max laughs. "Oh, come on! I'm sure we'd make do. Besides, in that universe, women probably evolved into something even more extraordinary."

Leah grins. "Nice save, Max. You're lucky this isn't that universe because I'd definitely be pulling the strings behind the scenes there, too."

Leah's expression grows more thoughtful, her playful tone softening. "You know, Max, it's almost unsettling to think how close that could have come to reality. If the government had allowed research like the one discovered in China in the early 21st century— the one where they managed to create a fertilized embryo with the cells of two male mice— it might have been only a matter of time before those experiments progressed to human cells. Who knows what kind of world that could have led to?"

She pauses, her voice more measured. "It's fascinating and a little terrifying how advancements in science can blur the lines of what we think is possible or even ethical. It makes you wonder just how many forks in the road humanity has faced that could've changed the course of everything."

Leah leans forward, her tone shifting into something more reflective. "You know, Max, it's not just the scientific implications that are unsettling. It's the culture and history that could've been lost along the way. Fertility and the role of women have been central to so many stories, traditions, and myths that define who we are."

She smiles softly. "Take Freya, for example—the goddess of fertility, love, and war. She's not just a figure from Norse mythology; she's a symbol of strength and protection, even in modern society. Remember the legend where Thor had to disguise himself as Freya to trick the giant Thrym into returning his hammer, Mjölnir? It's such a powerful metaphor for how fiercely she represents the readiness to safeguard her loved ones and the balance of the world."

Max leans back, his eyes narrowing in thought. "It's astounding to think how fragile the course of history is. Imagine if the liberal governments of the 20th century had prevailed—valuing individual freedoms over scientific advancement and collective progress. We might never have reached this point where eugenics reshaped humanity. A world where mental illness is no longer a struggle, cancer has been eradicated, and people live to 150 years, still vibrant and thriving."

He pauses, running his hand through his hair. "But would the cost of losing those advancements have been worth it? How much of our humanity, our values, would have been preserved in a world where personal liberty trumped control over the future? I wonder if there's a multiverse where that balance wasn't tipped toward progress at all costs."

His voice becomes quieter. "It's a reminder of the weight of choices— how societies evolve based on the ideals they champion and the sacrifices they're willing to make."

Leah pauses, her eyes shining with passion. "A world without women would lose not just the people, but the stories, the symbols, and the very fabric of cultural identity that figures like Freya embody. I think we underestimate how much of our humanity is rooted in the myths and values we've inherited from the past."

Max smiled and shifted the conversation to a brighter note. "You know, Leah, speaking of the future—it's hard not to get excited about the millennial celebration coming up in less than a decade. People from all over northern Europe are already preparing for it. The events, the music, the art—it's going to be unlike anything we've seen before. A true showcase of how far we've come as a society."

Leah's face lit up. "I've heard the plans are extraordinary. Cultural exhibitions, provincial collaborations—there's even talk of using holographic recreations to bring history to life. It'll be the celebration of an era, a unifying moment for everyone."

Max nodded enthusiastically. "Absolutely. A once-in-a-lifetime moment to reflect on our progress, our resilience, and to look ahead to the endless possibilities the future holds."

And with that, their conversation shifted to the anticipation of what was to come—an event that promised to celebrate the heart and soul of their shared heritage and dreams for tomorrow, an event that would mark the thousandth anniversary of the Reich.

Printed in Dunstable, United Kingdom